Daisy-Head Mayzie

By Dr. Seuss

HarperCollins *Children's Books*

The Cat in the Hat
™ & © Dr. Seuss Enterprises, L.P. 1957
All Rights Reserved

9 10 8

ISBN-13: 978-0-00-717521-5
ISBN-10: 0-00-717521-3

Based on the animated television special
Daisy-Head Mayzie,
produced by Hanna-Barbera Cartoons, Inc.,
in association with
Tony Collingwood Productions Ltd.

Daisy-Head Mayzie
© 1994 by Dr. Seuss Enterprises, L.P.
All Rights Reserved
First published in the UK 1996
This edition published in the UK 2004 by
HarperCollins*Children's Books,*
a division of HarperCollins*Publishers* Ltd
77-85 Fulham Palace Road
London W6 8JB

Visit our website at:
www.harpercollins.co.uk

Printed and bound in Hong Kong

It's hard to believe such a thing could be true,
And I hope such a thing never happens to you.
But it happened, they say, to poor Mayzie McGrew.
And it happened like this...

ROOM
8

She was sitting one day,
At her desk, in her school, in her usual way,
When she felt a small *twitch* on the top of her head.
So Mayzie looked up. And she almost dropped dead.
Something peculiar was going on there...

A daisy was sprouting right out of her hair!

Behind her was sitting young Herman (Butch) Stroodel.
"This looks like a daisy up here on her noodle!
It doesn't make sense! Why, it *couldn't* be so!
A noodle's no place for a daisy to grow!"

Then up spoke another boy, Einstein Van Tass,
The brightest young man in the whole of the class,
"It's a very odd place to be sprouting a daisy.
But, nevertheless, one IS growing on Mayzie!"

"Hey! Lookit," cried Butch, "right here in this room!
Daisy-Head Mayzie! She's bursting in bloom."

Miss Sneetcher, the teacher, came rushing up quick.
"Such nonsense! Some child here is playing a trick!
Which one of you boys stuck that thing in her hair?
You *know* that a daisy could never grow there!"

"But, Teacher," said Butch, "I saw the thing rise
Right out of her head with my very own eyes.
Just give it a yank if you think I tell lies!"

But Miss Sneetcher had heard quite enough of this talk.
"Mayzie! Hold still! Let me get at that stalk!"

"OUCH!" hollered Mayzie.

"Quit yanking," Butch said. "You're giving her pains.
I'll bet that those roots go way down in her brains!"

The kids in the class started shouting like crazy:
"Daisy-Head! Daisy-Head! DAISY-HEAD MAYZIE!"

"Children, be quiet! Good grief and alas!"
Miss Sneetcher was shocked by the noise in her class.
"I've taught in this room twenty years. Maybe more.
But I've never seen anything like this before!
I'll have to report it. You'll just have to come
To the Principal's office and show Mr. Grumm!"

Now the Principal, good Mr. Gregory Grumm,
Was a very wise man, just as smart as they come.
He knew more than anyone else in this nation
About long division and multiplication.
He knew all the answers. Why oceans are deep.
Why skies are so high, and why mountains are steep.
He should have the answer to this thing on Mayzie.

"My word!" he declared. "It's a genuine daisy!
I've seen them quite often in fields growing wild.
But never before on the head of a child.
Now what in the world ever made this thing sprout?
I have no idea. But I'm going to find out!

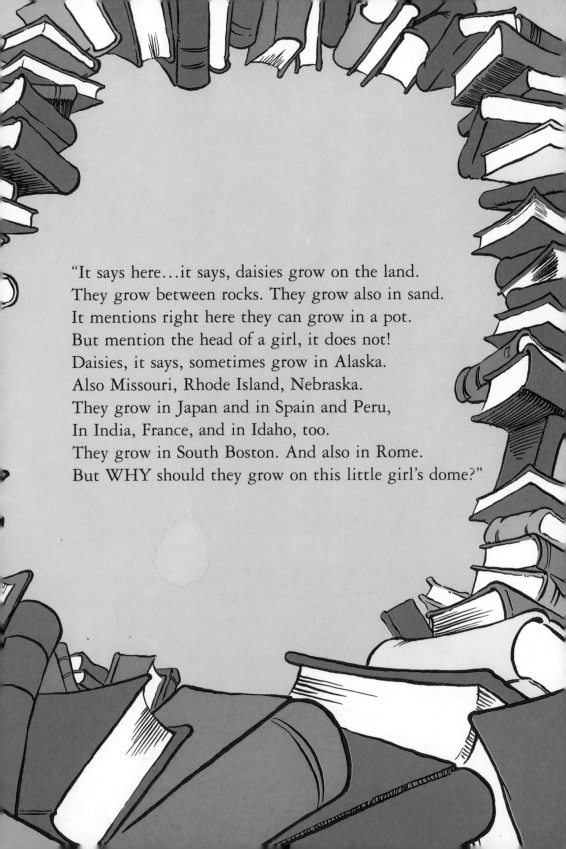

"It says here…it says, daisies grow on the land.
They grow between rocks. They grow also in sand.
It mentions right here they can grow in a pot.
But mention the head of a girl, it does not!
Daisies, it says, sometimes grow in Alaska.
Also Missouri, Rhode Island, Nebraska.
They grow in Japan and in Spain and Peru,
In India, France, and in Idaho, too.
They grow in South Boston. And also in Rome.
But WHY should they grow on this little girl's dome?"

"Say, lookit!" said Mayzie.

"It's wilting! It's drooping! How wonderful, Mayzie!
It soon will be dead! You'll be rid of that daisy!"

"In just a few minutes, our troubles will pass,"
Declared Mr. Grumm. "Take her back to the class."

Then the principal saw a most terrible sight.
The daisy was dying. (And THAT was all right.)
But that daisy was part of poor Mayzie McGrew,
And Mayzie was starting to wilt away, too!
"Teacher," said Grumm, "you know what I think...!
They're *both* going to die! Hurry! Bring them a drink!"

"That daisy! That girl's the worst problem in town!
You take her away and you make her lie down!
You lock her up tight in that room down the hall.
There are quite a few numbers that I've got to call!"

"Get Mayzie's parents on the end of the line.
I need them here quickly while there is still time!"

On the phone Mayzie's mom asked, "What's all the fuss?"
Then: "Goodness to Betsy! I'll catch the next bus!"

A call to the shoe store reached Mr. McGrew.
He answered while holding a customer's shoe.
"Yes, this is…Oh, no!
I really must go!"

"A doctor should see her," the Principal said,
"And an expert on plants like the one on her head."

So he called Dr. Eisenbart, who said, "What a trick!
My stethoscope's packed, I'll be there in a tick!"

"Wait, Doc!" said his patient, "I'll come along too.
My brother's a vet. And he knows this McGrew."

When he heard, Finch the Florist grabbed for his shears,
"I'll be there just as soon as my truck can shift gears!"

Meanwhile, poor Mayzie lay down on a couch,
The daisy slumped down on its leaves in a slouch.
But the window was open, because it was warm,
And the sweet-smelling daisy attracted a swarm
Of bees.

The faster she ran,
The faster they flew.
So Mayzie kept running.
What else could she do?

She attempted to hide behind Officer Thatcher,
Who cupped out his hat like a bumblebee catcher.
The bees took his hat.
Thatcher said, "I'm no fool!"
And ran after Mayzie back to the school.

Principal Grumm didn't know what to do.

"It's worse!" cried Miss Sneetcher. "Much worse than we feared.
The daisy and Mayzie have both disappeared!"

Behind her came charging Mr. McGrew,
Chased by a customer chasing his shoe,
Finch the Florist, Dr. Eisenbart, too.
Dr. Eisenbart's patient, and Mrs. McGrew.

Then through the window with Officer Thatcher,
Who slammed the pane shut so the bees couldn't catch her,
Jumped Mayzie McGrew
To the floor in a splatter,
With the daisy still there, except taller and fatter!

"My poor little daughter! The daisy! It's true!
I'm going to faint!" cried Mrs. McGrew.

"Tut, tut," said the Florist, "there's no need for tears
Just because there's a daisy between her two ears.
I'll snip it right off with my sharp pruning shears."

"She's *my* patient, don't touch her! You must stand apart!
We have to have room," said Doc Eisenbart.
"I think that Mayzie and her plant
Could help *me* get a research grant!"

Then the door opened wide
And the Mayor stepped inside.
At meetings and greetings there was none to compare.
He was best at long speeches, chock-full of hot air!
"I promise, my friends, that if I'm re-elected,
This daisy on Mayzie will be disconnected.
The law of our fathers is simple and sound,
Daisies belong and should stay in the ground.
The rest are illegal. We'll bar them from town!"

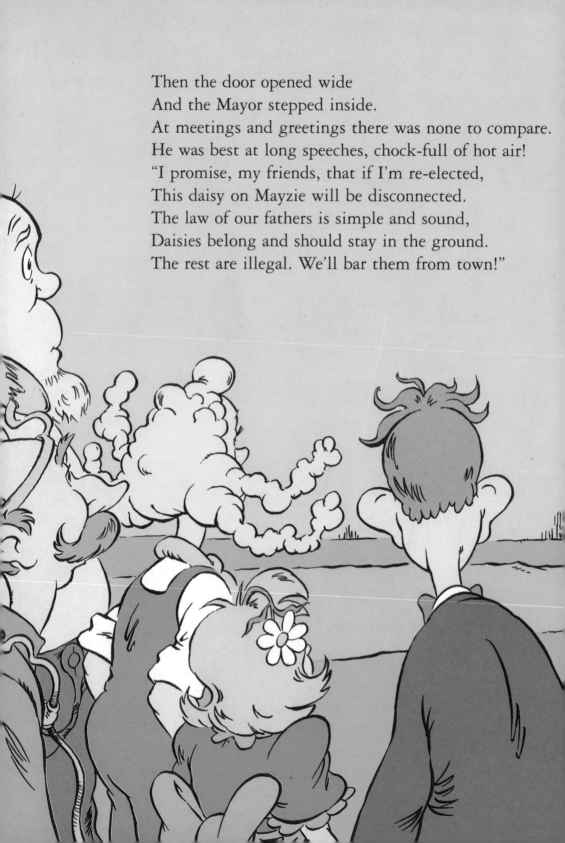

From the back came a voice, sometimes loud, sometimes slick,
Of a wheeler and dealer, who knew every trick!
"I'm Finagle the Agent. You've heard of me, I'm sure.
I represent young what's-his-name, and others, now on tour.
But, Mayzie, you're so special, please let me shake your hand.
Your talent is a wondrous thing—unique in all the land.
'Daisy-Head Mayzie' spelled out in bright light
Will draw kids in the day, and parents at night!
Daisy-Head Mayzie, you've got quite an act!
Just stick with me, kid,
And sign this contract.
          Your flower needs to sign too."

Her mother said, "Mayzie! Don't be a fool!"
And the Principal begged her not to leave school.
But Mayzie didn't stop to blink.
She signed her name in think-proof ink.

And the daisy signed too.

Daisy-Head fever was gripping the nation.
It had quickly become a worldwide sensation!

Daisy-Head burgers,
And Daisy-Head drinks.
Daisy-Head stockings,
And Daisy-Head sinks.
Daisy-Head buttons,
And Daisy-Head bows.
Mayzie was famous,
The star of her shows.

Fame had knocked on Mayzie's door.
Now she had it all—and more.
Piles of money stacked in tens,

But what is money without friends?
A dream had led her far astray.
That was the price she had to pay.

Mayzie McGrew ran night and day,
Nowhere to go, nowhere to stay.
Because she was sure that everyone must
Have written her off in total disgust,
Over and over again in her head,
These are the words that poor Mayzie said:
"I can never go home. Nobody loves me.
Nobody loves me. Nobody loves me."

Nobody loved her...? Poor Mayzie McGrew!
It's hard to believe such a thing could be true.
And maybe that's why, then, this daisy above,
When Mayzie, below, began talking of love...
Well, you know about daisies.
When love is in doubt,
The job of a daisy is, Try and Find Out!

They love her...
They love her NOT!
They love her...
They love her NOT!

Don't worry, Mayzie.
They love you.

"They love me!"

Well...

That's how it all happened. The thing went away.
And Mayzie McGrew is quite happy today,
Back at her studies, and doing just great
In all of her subjects in Room Number 8.

And concerning that daisy...you know that it *never*
Grew out of the top of her head again *ever!*

Errr…well, it *practically* never popped up there again.
Excepting, occasionally. Just now and then.

TING!

"And, after all...*I'm* getting used to it!"

Read them **together**, read them **alone**, read them **aloud** and make **reading fun!**
With over **30 wacky stories** to choose from, now it's **easier** than **ever** to find the
right **Dr. Seuss** books for your child – just let the **back cover colour** guide you!

Blue back books
for sharing with your child

Dr. Seuss' ABC
The Foot Book
Hop on Pop
Mr. Brown Can Moo! Can You?
One Fish, Two Fish, Red Fish, Blue Fish
There's a Wocket in my Pocket!

Green back books
for children just beginning to read on their own

And to Think That I Saw It on Mulberry Street
The Cat in the Hat
The Cat in the Hat Comes Back
Fox in Socks
Green Eggs and Ham
I Can Read With My Eyes Shut!
I Wish That I Had Duck Feet
Marvin K. Mooney Will You Please Go Now!
Oh, Say Can You Say?
Oh, the Thinks You Can Think!
Ten Apples Up on Top
Wacky Wednesday
Hunches in Bunches
Happy Birthday to YOU

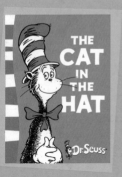

Yellow back books
for fluent readers to enjoy

Daisy-Head Mayzie
Did I Ever Tell You How Lucky You Are?
Dr. Seuss' Sleep Book
Horton Hatches the Egg
Horton Hears a Who!
How the Grinch Stole Christmas!
If I Ran the Circus
If I Ran the Zoo
I Had Trouble in Getting to Solla Sollew
The Lorax
Oh, the Places You'll Go!
On Beyond Zebra
Scrambled Eggs Super!
The Sneetches and other stories
Thidwick the Big-Hearted Moose
Yertle the Turtle and other stories